First published in Belgium and Holland by Clavis Uitgeverij, Hasselt – Amsterdam, 2015
Copyright © 2015, Clavis Uitgeverij

English translation from the Dutch by Clavis Publishing Inc. New York
Copyright © 2016 for the English language edition: Clavis Publishing Inc. New York

Visit us on the web at www.clavisbooks.com

I'll Be a Cowboy written and illustrated by Anita Bijsterbosch
Original title: *Ik ga als cowboy*
Translated from the Dutch by Clavis Publishing

ISBN 978-1-60537-277-8

This book was printed in January 2016 at Wai Man Book Binding (China) Ltd. Flat A, 9/F, Phase 1,
Kwun Tong Industrial Centre, 472-484 Kwun Tong Road, Kwun Tong, Kowloon, H.K.

First Edition
10 9 8 7 6 5 4 3 2 1

Clavis Publishing supports the First Amendment and celebrates the right to read

I'll Be a
COWBOY

Anita Bijsterbosch

Clavis

NEW YORK

"Mommy, there's a party at school tomorrow, and we get to wear costumes!" Sammy says.

"I think I'll be a *cowboy*."

horse

lasso

cowboy hat

shirt

kerchief

vest

belt

fringed pants

spurs

cowboy boots

"Yee-Haw!"

"Or wait, I'll go as a *firefighter.*"

dragon

walkie-talkie

fire engine

flashlight

helmet

firefighter suit

gloves

firefighter boots

"Fire!"

"Hmm, perhaps I'll be a *pirate*."

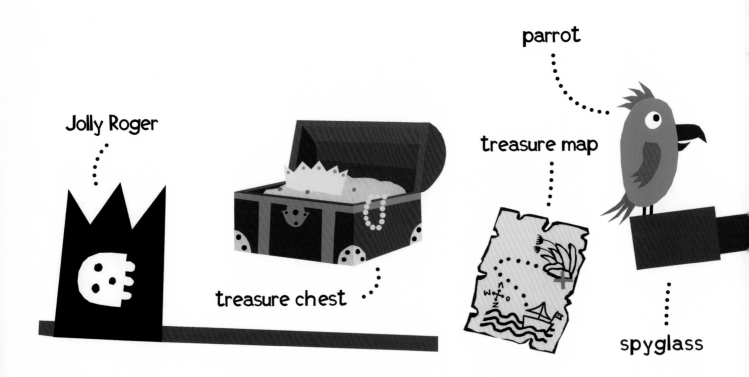

Jolly Roger

treasure chest

treasure map

parrot

spyglass

bandana

eye patch

striped T-shirt

belt

cutlass

trousers

buccaneer
boots

"Land ho!"

"Or I could go as a *knight*."

castle

horse

cuddly toy

feather

dragon

sword

helmet

armor

gauntlet

shield

boots

"Tan-tan-tara!"

"I could be a *magician*..."

wand

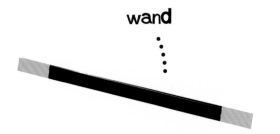

magic hat

robe

boots

"Or maybe
I should
just go
as *myself?*"